My Day
with
Gong Gong

words by
Sennah Yee

pictures by
Elaine Chen

annick press
toronto • berkeley

Mom is dropping me off at my Gong Gong's house for the day.

"I wish you could stay with me," I say.
What will Gong Gong and I talk about?
I don't know Chinese . . .

"It will be okay, May," says Mom. "You will still have fun!"

I don't know about that!

Gong Gong is watching hockey on TV. **Boring!**

Gong Gong must think so too, because he's asleep.

I change the channel to a cartoon.

Gong Gong wakes up and smiles. He turns off the TV.

Hey! I wanted to keep watching!

He gets up and puts on his old cap and his puffy vest.
It's time for a walk.

Gong Gong's neighbor waves at us.

"*Nei hou!*" says Gong Gong.

His neighbor says something in Chinese.
Gong Gong laughs and points at me.

Huh? What's so funny?

Down the street, vendors sell jewelry
and toys, and a man plays Chinese violin.

Inside a gift shop, the cashier waves at us.

"*Nei hou!*" he says.
He chats with Gong Gong in Chinese.

I look at the glass counter display:
jade earrings, cotton slippers,
and small toy animals.

The monkey is my favorite,
because it's my Chinese zodiac sign.

My tummy grumbles.
I pull on Gong Gong's sleeve.

"Can we eat?" I ask.

He pats my head and smiles,
but that's not what I asked for!

Gong Gong takes us to a dim sum restaurant next.
Maybe he understood me after all.

"*Nei hou!*" says Gong Gong.

The cooks nod back as they wrap
dumplings with their hands.

Carts of food pass by me: yummy pork buns, fried turnip cake, mango pudding . . . **I'm so hungry!**

"Can we eat?" I ask Gong Gong again. But he only orders tea.

Next is the supermarket.
Gong Gong buys groceries:
fish, tofu, and vegetables.

"*Mm goi,*" says Gong Gong when
the cashier hands him his bags.

I help Gong Gong carry them—
they're heavy!

I hope we eat soon.

Chinatown is always busy.
Cars, streetcars, and bicycles zoom by.

When it's time to cross the street,
Gong Gong holds my hand.

Everyone is in a rush.

I pull on Gong Gong's hand, but he's a pretty
slow walker, so I have to slow down, too.

I wish he'd hurry up!

Gong Gong's friends are playing cards and feeding pigeons in the park.

I thought we were going home to eat!

Gong Gong gives me some cards. His friends look at me and smile.

"Dak yi," says one of his friends.

They all laugh, but I'm not
doing anything funny!

I can't understand Gong Gong's friends, I don't know how
to play this game, and we've been sitting here for so long!

I throw down my cards. Pigeons keep poking at crumbs near my feet.

"Go away!" I yell. I stomp and run through them and they all fly away.

Eww!
A pigeon pooped
on my coat!

"*Aiya!*" Gong Gong and his friends laugh when they see my poopy coat.

I cover my face and cry.

Gong Gong stops laughing.

He walks over and reaches into his pocket.
He takes out a tissue and helps me clean off the poop.

He reaches into another pocket and gives me two small bags.

It's the toy monkey from the gift shop!

How did Gong Gong know that's the one I wanted?

I open the other small bag.
Pork buns from the dim sum restaurant!

How did Gong Gong know these are my favorite?

"Thank you! *Doh je!*" I say.

Gong Gong smiles.

We sit by the water fountain
and eat the pork buns.

Some pigeons try to eat our crumbs.

Gong Gong stands up and waves his arms to scare them away for me.

It's getting dark and cold.
Gong Gong zips up my coat.

"Let's go," I say.

Gong Gong looks at me.

I point to the street. "Home," I say.

Gong Gong nods. "Home."

Everyone is still in a rush.

I hold Gong Gong's hand.

We take our time.

"*Nei hou*, May!" says the cashier.

Hey, that's me!

"*Nei hou!*" I say.

"Doh je!" I say.

More buns, yummy!

I make my toy monkey do a funny dance.

The cashier makes the other toys in the window dance, too.

Gong Gong gives me a coin and points. I drop the coin in the man's violin case.

"Doh jeh!" he says.

Mom is back to pick me up
from Gong Gong's house.

"Did you have fun?"

I show her my toy monkey.

"Aw, so cute! *Dak yi!*" she laughs and says
something to Gong Gong in Chinese.

I don't know what she said, but
Gong Gong laughs, so I do, too.

"Bye-bye, May," says Gong Gong. *"Ngo oi nei!"*

"What does that mean?" I ask Mom.

"It means 'I love you,'" says Mom.

I give Gong Gong a big hug.

"Bye, Gong Gong!" I say. *"Ngo oi nei!"*

May and Gong Gong's Cantonese

得意 = *dak yi* = cute

多謝 = *doh je* = thank you (when receiving a gift)

公公 = *gong gong* = grandpa (mother's side)

唔該 = *mm goi* = thank you (when receiving help)

你好 = *nei hou* = hello

我愛你 = *ngo oi nei* = I love you

Cover art by Elaine Chen, designed by Paul Covello
Interior design by Paul Covello

Annick Press Ltd.

We acknowledge the support of the Canada Council for the Arts and the Ontario Arts Council, and the participation of the Government of Canada/la participation du gouvernement du Canada for our publishing activities.

Library and Archives Canada Cataloguing in Publication

Title: My day with Gong Gong / words by Sennah Yee ; pictures by Elaine Chen.
Names: Yee, Sennah, 1992- author. | Chen, Elaine, 1991- illustrator.
Description: Text in English; includes some text in Chinese.
Identifiers: Canadiana (print) 20200189026 | Canadiana (ebook) 20200189042 | ISBN 9781773214290 (hardcover) | ISBN 9781773214283 (softcover) | ISBN 9781773214313 (PDF) | ISBN 9781773214306 (HTML) | ISBN 9781773214597 (Kindle)
Classification: LCC PS8647.E45 M9 2020 | DDC jC813/.6—dc23

Published in the U.S.A. by Annick Press (U.S.) Ltd.
Distributed in Canada by University of Toronto Press.
Distributed in the U.S.A. by Publishers Group West.

Printed in China

annickpress.com   sennahyee.com   elainechen.ca

Also available as an e-book. Please visit annickpress.com/ebooks for more details.